bloated

boast

celebrate

huff

lumber

mumbled

prepare

scamper

stretching

trudge

www.rourkeeducationalmedia.com

Edited by Luana K. Mitten
Illustrated by Bob Reese
Art Direction and Page Layout by Renee Brady

Library of Congress Cataloging-in-Publication Data

Steinkraus, Kyla
 Ready, Set, RACE! / Kyla Steinkraus.
    p. cm. -- (Little Birdie Books)
 ISBN 978-1-61741-829-7(hard cover) (alk. paper)
 ISBN 978-1-61236-033-1 (soft cover)
 Library of Congress Control Number: 2011924712

Printed in China, FOFO I - Production Company
  Shenzhen, Guangdong Province

rourkeeducationalmedia.com

customerservice@rourkeeducationalmedia.com • PO Box 643328 Vero Beach, Florida 32964

Ready, Set, RACE!

By Kyla Steinkraus
Illustrated by Bob Reese

The forest was buzzing with excitement. Oswald Owl had just announced that the first prize for the annual Great Race would be a wonderful party. Everyone wanted the prize, but there could only be one winner.

"I'll be first," boasted Freddy Fox. "My long legs make me the fastest."

Tonya Turtle frowned. "My legs are much too short to be quick."

"Don't worry," Barry Beaver said. "We can practice to get faster."

"We'd better start soon. The race is in three days!" cried Debbie Duck.

The friends hurried off to prepare.

But Freddy didn't need to prepare. He was already the fastest.

The animals marked off a track. They practiced racing again and again. "Train with us!" called Tonya Turtle.

But Freddy felt like curling up to take a nap in the sun. So he did.

The next day, Bella Bear gave the friends fruit to eat.

"Healthy food will give us energy," she said. Debbie Duck offered Freddy a banana.

But Freddy felt like eating ice cream instead. So he did.

After he finished, Freddy Fox's stomach was very bloated. He trudged over to his friends.

"We're stretching," huffed Barry Beaver as he reached for his toes.

Debbie Duck lifted her wings over her head as high as she could. "You might hurt your muscles if you don't stretch."

Freddy shook his head and sat down. Stretching looked like a lot of work. "I think I'll just watch," he mumbled. So he did.

At last it was time for the race. All the animals stood in a row behind the starting line. "Ready, set, race!" yelled Oswald Owl.

Freddy Fox leaped ahead. After awhile, his stomach began to hurt from all that ice cream. Bella Bear lumbered past him.

He ran on. Soon his lungs ached. He couldn't breathe. Debbie Duck flapped ahead of him.

Freddy stumbled. His paws cramped.

Barry Beaver scooped up Tonya Turtle. Together they scampered ahead of Freddy and across the finish line.

Freddy hung his head as he limped to the end of the race. He had lost!

Freddy crept away as his friends cheered for Bella Bear.

"Wait!" Bella called. "Come celebrate with us!"

"Yeah," Tonya Turtle chimed in. "There's plenty of ice cream."

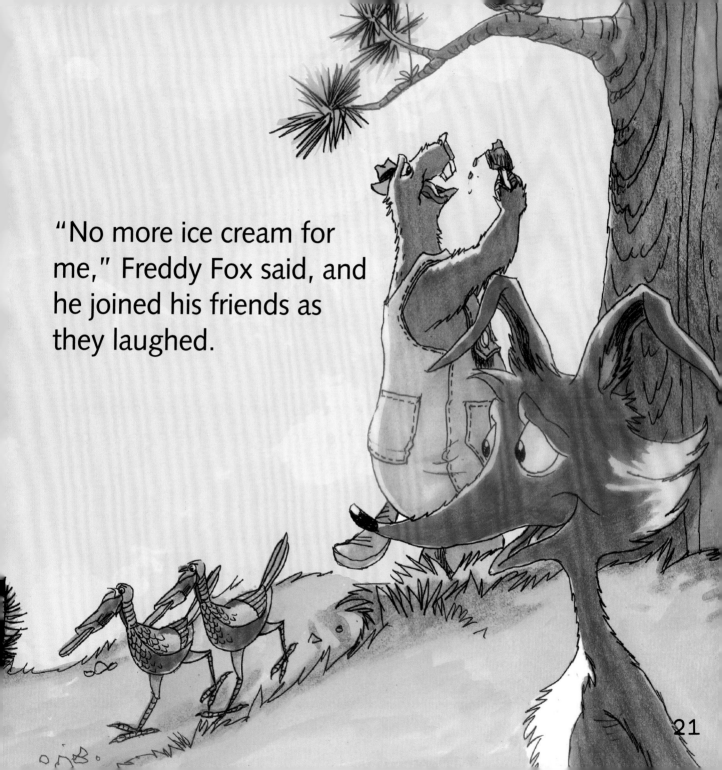

"No more ice cream for me," Freddy Fox said, and he joined his friends as they laughed.

21

After Reading Activities

You and the Story...

What did Freddy Fox do to prepare for the race?

What did the rest of the animals do to prepare for the race?

What would you do to prepare for a big race?

Words You Know Now...

Choose three of the words below and write them on a piece of paper. Now write a definition in your own words for each of the three words you chose.

bloated	mumbled
boast	prepare
celebrate	scamper
huff	stretching
lumber	trudge

You Could... Arrange to Have a Big Race with Friends

- Invite your friends to be a part of your race.

- Decide when and where the race will be held.

- Make a list of things that you can do to prepare for the race.

- Decide what you will do to celebrate the winner of the race.

About the Author

Kyla Steinkraus lives in Tampa with her husband and two children. She believes exercising, stretching, and eating healthy are great ways to prepare not just for racing, but for life, too.

About the Artist

Bob Reese began his art career at age 17 working for Walt Disney Studio. His projects included the animated feature films Sleeping Beauty, The Sword and the Stone, and Paul Bunyan. He has also worked for Bob Clampett and Hanna Barbera Studios. He resides in Utah and enjoys spending time with his two daughters, five grandchildren, and cat named Venus.

Comprehension & Extension:

- Retell the Story: Five Boxes

  Have five pieces of paper. Ask the class to tell you five important things that happened in the story. Write each response on one of the pieces of paper. Have five children hold the papers and have the class work together to put the five important events in the correct sequence.

- Text to Self Connection:

  Tell a friend of a time when you were in a race. Did you win the race or lose the race? Tell how you felt at the end of the race.

- Extension: Continue the Text

  Pretend that the story continues on. Write another chapter about what Freddy Fox will do before the next race.

Sight Words I Used:

after
again
could
don't
first
give
just
off

Words to Know:

(See activity on page 22.)

Little Birdie Books

Ready, Set, RACE!

Vibrant illustrations and engaging leveled text in Little Birdie Books' Leveled Readers work together to tell fun stories while supporting your transitioning readers. Before reading vocabulary building and after reading activities develop young readers' vocabulary and reading comprehension.

ISBN 978-1-61236-033-1

90000

9 781612 360331

Printed in China

Rourke
Educational Media

rourkeeducationalmedia.com

T1-BJA-673